Bala Kids
An imprint of Shambhala Publications, Inc.
2129 13th Street
Boulder, Colorado 80302
www.shambhala.com

9 8 7 6 5 4 3 2 1

First Edition
Printed in China

Shambhala Publications makes every effort to print on acid-free,
recycled paper.
Bala Kids is distributed worldwide by Penguin Random House, Inc.,
and its subsidiaries.

Designed by John Ledda
Art Directed by Kara Plikaitis

Library of Congress Cataloging-in-Publication Data
Names: Hampton, Francesca, author. | Ledda, John, illustrator.
Title: Leo learns to meditate / Francesca Hampton; illustrated by
John Ledda.
Description: Boulder: Shambhala, 2022.
Identifiers: LCCN 2021001968 | ISBN 9781611809169 (hardback)
Subjects: LCSH: Meditation—Juvenile literature. | Meditation for
children.
Classification: LCC BF637.M4 H36 2021 | DDC 158.1/28—dc23
LC record available at https://lccn.loc.gov/2021001968

LEO LEARNS TO
MEDITATE

A Curious Kid's Guide to Life's Ups and Downs and Lots In-Between

FRANCESCA HAMPTON

illustrated by
JOHN LEDDA

bala kids

MAYBE YOU'LL FIND THIS STRANGE, BUT IN MY FAMILY, EVERYONE "MEDITATES" BUT ME. BUT WHAT IS **MEDITATE?**

TRY TO THINK ABOUT TEDDY FOR ONE MINUTE.
HA! THIS IS GOING TO BE TOTALLY EASY. I CLOSE MY EYES AND I THINK...
TEDDY, TEDDY, TEDDY, EDDY, EDDY, EDDY, DEDDY...
I WONDER WHAT LUPITA IS HAVING FOR BREAKFAST!
TEDDY, EDDY... OUR TEACHER WORE FUNNY SHOES YESTERDAY— THEY WERE PURPLE!
TEDDY, EDDY, EDDY...
LUNCH! PEANUT BUTTER, JELLY! TELLY, TEDDY, WEDDY, BEDDY—
DARN IT! TEDDY!

MOM CONSIDERS MY WORDS. I LIKE THAT SHE IS ALWAYS A GOOD LISTENER.
IN THE BEGINNING, MEDITATION CAN SEEM BORING. BUT IF YOU DO IT CORRECTLY, LITTLE BY LITTLE, YOU WILL FIND THAT IT'S NOT BORING.
MEDITATION CAN MAKE YOU ***CALMER*** AND ***WISER*** AND ***KINDER***.
BUT ALL THIS BEGINS WITH SIMPLY BEING QUIET INSIDE AND CLEARLY FOCUSING ON ONE THING AT A TIME.

AND SO THAT VERY DAY, RIGHT AFTER SCHOOL—AND A SNACK—I START LEARNING HOW TO MEDITATE.
SIT CROSS-LEGGED, WITH YOUR BACK STRAIGHT AND YOUR CHIN SLIGHTLY DOWN—BUT RELAXED.
IMAGINE YOU'RE A PUPPET AND SOMEONE'S HOLDING YOU UP WITH A STRING.
I CAN DO THAT.

PUT YOUR HANDS IN YOUR LAP, YOUR RIGHT HAND RESTING ON YOUR LEFT HAND AND THE TIPS OF YOUR THUMBS JUST TOUCHING.
I CAN DO THAT.
CLOSE YOUR EYES HALFWAY. LOOK DOWN IN FRONT OF YOU, BUT DON'T FOCUS YOUR EYES. YOU CAN CLOSE THEM SOMETIMES IF YOU WANT.
I LOOK OVER AT TEDDY—HE'S ALREADY DOING IT JUST RIGHT.

MY LEGS **DO** FEEL NICE AND LIGHT. EVERY PART OF THEM. THEY FEEL CALM. I TAKE TURNS TIGHTENING AND RELAXING MY BELLY, SHOULDERS, AND ARMS.

I EVEN SQUINCH UP MY FACE AND RELAX IT.

THE NEXT AFTERNOON:

TODAY I WANT YOU TO FOCUS ON YOUR BREATHING.

I TAKE A GIANT BREATH AND HOLD IT.

NO, NO. JUST BREATHE NORMALLY.

PAY ATTENTION TO THE AIR COMING IN AND OUT OF YOUR NOSE.

FEEL YOUR BELLY RISE AND FALL.

I CAN DO THAT. MY MIND MOVES DOWN TO MY BELLY AND FEELS IT GO UP AND DOWN. I START TO NOTICE THE COOL AIR COMING INTO MY NOSE AND THE WARM AIR GOING OUT.

COUNT TO TEN AS YOU BREATHE, COUNTING EACH FULL BREATH AS ONE.

I START COUNTING TO TEN. ONE... TWO...

BUT SOMETHING FUNNY IS HAPPENING.

MY BREATH IS GOING SLOWER AND SLOWER. PRETTY SOON, THERE IS SO MUCH TIME BETWEEN THE NUMBERS, I KIND OF FORGET TO COUNT.

MY MIND HAS GONE SOMEWHERE ELSE.

WHERE DID IT GO?

OH, THERE IT IS!

PUSHING TOO HARD CAN CAUSE YOUR THOUGHTS TO FLY EVERY WHICH WAY, LIKE SEAGULLS WHEN YOU ARE THROWING THEM BREAD.

SERIOUSLY? SO MUCH TO REMEMBER! BUT I TAKE A DEEP BREATH, AND I SHUT MY EYES AGAIN.

BREATHE IN. RELAX. BE MINDFUL.

BREATHE OUT. RELAX.

BREATHE IN...

AND THEN I FALL ASLEEP!

I WAKE UP TO MOM LAUGHING.
MEDITATING *JUST RIGHT* IS HARDER THAN IT LOOKS, ISN'T IT? BUT YOU CAN DO IT.
THINK ABOUT WHEN DADDY PLAYS HIS GUITAR.
IF HE MAKES THE STRINGS TOO TIGHT, THEY SOUND SQUEAKY AND CAN EVEN BREAK. AND IF HE MAKES THEM TOO LOOSE, THEY'LL JUST BE FLOPPY AND WON'T MAKE ANY SOUND.
BUT IF HE TIGHTENS THEM *JUST RIGHT*, THEY CAN MAKE THE MOST BEAUTIFUL MUSIC IN THE WORLD.
A PERSON WHO IS MEDITATING *JUST RIGHT* IS PAYING ATTENTION, GENTLY BUT WITH CLARITY...
... NOT TOO TIGHT, NOT TOO LOOSE.

APRIL
14
SO I TRY AGAIN, EVERY DAY AFTER SCHOOL. IT'S BEEN TWO WEEKS, AND I CAN FOCUS CLEARLY ON MY BREATH NOW, WITHOUT GETTING TENSE OR TRYING TOO HARD, SOMETIMES FOR EVEN A MINUTE!
GOOD! IT IS BETTER TO MEDITATE WELL THAN TO MEDITATE FOR A LONG TIME. IF YOU FEEL SLEEPY, STOP.
BUT NOW I ALMOST NEVER FALL ASLEEP! AND THE NICEST PART IS FEELING SO GOOD AND PEACEFUL AT THE END OF MEDITATING.
APRIL
10
MOST OF THE TIME.
APRIL
5
APRIL
7

THEN SHERMAN **PUNCHES** ME IN THE NOSE!

I HOPE HE FEELS *TERRIBLE!*
NOT YOU?
SOME PEOPLE WOULD SAY THAT IS A VERY NORMAL WAY TO FEEL.
I THINK YOU CAN DO BETTER, IF YOU TRY.
SHERMAN GOT IN A LOT OF TROUBLE TODAY, AT SCHOOL AND AT HOME. AND HE DIDN'T EVEN GET TO TASTE YOUR PIE. IN FACT, ANOTHER PARENT TOLD ME SOMETIMES HE COMES TO SCHOOL WITHOUT ANY LUNCH TO EAT AT ALL.
LEO, CAN YOU IMAGINE BEING HUNGRY AND SEEING ANOTHER BOY EATING A BIG PIECE OF JUICY PIE?
HOW WOULD YOU FEEL?

I TAKE ANOTHER BIG, SLOW BREATH AND LET IT GO.

AND THEN A FEW MORE.

I START TO CALM DOWN.

BASIC MINDFULNESS MEDITATION WITH LOVING KINDNESS

Buddhism contains a wealth of profound reflective practices to explore. Below is a simple meditation for beginners that gives a first taste of developing mindful awareness and compassion. Along with wisdom, these form the heart of all Buddhist practices. My Tibetan teachers have always told me that beginners should keep meditations short. Ten minutes per session is plenty and twenty minutes is maximum. If a youngster is ready to do more, it's advised to do so under the guidance of an experienced teacher. The following meditation can either be guided by an adult reading the steps aloud, or self-guided if the reading level of the young meditator is sufficient.

1. **Now it's time to do our meditation.** To help our mind become calm, loving, and clear, we give ourselves permission not to be in a hurry for this time, and not to worry about anything else.

2. **Sit cross-legged,** on a floor cushion or in a chair, or lie down on your back. Keep your back straight and your body relaxed. If you are sitting, it can help to imagine you are a puppet and someone is holding you up straight with strings! Cross your legs and rest your hands in your lap with the right hand on top of the left hand, facing up. Let the tips of your thumbs touch each other.

3. **Now close your eyes partway.** Drop your chin a little and look down at the floor in front of you. Don't focus your eyes; just relax them. You can even close them if it feels better.

4. **Take your mind down to your feet.** What are they doing? How do they feel right now? Are they touching anything? Tighten the muscles in your feet. Scrunch your toes and hold! Now relax them completely. How do your feet and lower legs feel? Notice every detail.

5. **Now move up your body, part by part.** You can flex and release or just focus on relaxing each part, even your face! Rest in that relaxed feeling. Let your whole body feel soft and creamy with no tension anywhere.

6. **Now focus your mind on your breath.** Feel the sensation your breath makes coming into your nose. Then feel it going out. Don't try to change your breathing. You can also focus on your stomach. Let it rise and fall naturally.

7. **What is your mind doing?** Are other thoughts carrying your attention away? This is normal. Whenever you notice this, gently let those thoughts go. You can think them later. Come back to your breathing.

8. **Notice if your mind is getting sleepy or dull.** Open your eyes wide for a moment if necessary and try to focus on your breath clearly again.

9. **Now imagine that you are loved so much.** Imagine that all the things you need to be safe and happy are coming to you. You have everything you want. Rest your mind in that feeling for a while.

10. **Now think of someone you love,** animal or human, who may be feeling sad or scared or really need something they don't have. What would make them happier? Make the strong wish inside: May they have it and be happy. May they be free from feeling bad or hurt in any way.

11. **Imagine that your feeling of loving kindness** is a warm light that fills you up. Send that loving light out to fill up the person or animal, and give them everything they need. Then keep going past that, extending the love to other people or animals you know. How far can you go? Keep going, bigger and bigger, out to as many beings as you can. Visualize that they are really starting to feel so joyful and peaceful. Rest your mind in your loving kindness light and feel happy for all the joy you have wished for others. May they really receive it.

12. **Now for dedication.** When we grow loving kindness in ourselves like this, it can have many good effects in our future. Imagine what you want those effects to be. Especially make the wish that your meditation will make you more and more able to be calm and peaceful and to help other beings with your wisdom and kindness as you get older.